To

From

A LITTLE SPOONFUL OF
CHICKEN SOUP FOR
THE MOTHER'S SOUL

Published by Blessings Unlimited, Pentagon Towers
P.O. Box 398004, Edina, MN 55439

Photo by Carolyn Parker/FPG
Design by Kim Hokanson

ISBN 1-58375-434-2
Printed in Mexico

A
Little
Spoonful
of

Chicken
Soup for the
Mother's
Soul

Love Notes

From the time each of my children started school, I packed their lunches. And in each lunch I packed, I included a note. Often written on a napkin, the note might be a thank-you for a special moment, a reminder of something we were happily anticipating, or a bit of encouragement for an upcoming test or sporting event.

In early grade school they loved their notes. But as kids grow older they become more self-conscious, and by the time he reached high school, my older son, Marc, informed me he no longer needed my daily missives. Informing him that they had been written as much for me as for him, and that he no longer needed to read them but I still needed to write them, I continued the tradition until the day he graduated.

Six years after high school graduation, Marc called and asked if he could move home for a couple of months. He had spent those years well, graduating from college, completing two congressional internships and finally, becoming a legislative assistant. With his younger sister leaving for college, I was especially thrilled to have him coming home.

A couple weeks after Marc arrived home he was back at work. Since I was still making lunch every day for his younger brother, I packed one for Marc, too. Imagine my surprise when I got a call from my 24-year-old son, complaining about his lunch.

"Did I do something wrong? Aren't I still your kid? Don't you love me any more, Mom?" were just a few of the queries he threw at me as I laughingly asked him what was wrong.

"My note, Mom," he answered. "Where's my note?"

— Antoinette Kuritz
Chicken Soup for the Mother's Soul

Forever, For Always,
and
No Matter What

Our daughter Ariana moved from baby to toddler with her share of the usual bumps and scraped knees. On these occasions, I'd hold out my arms and say, "Come see me." She'd crawl into my lap, we'd cuddle, and I'd say, "Are you my girl?" Between tears she'd nod her head yes. Then I'd say, "My sweetie, beetie Ariana girl?" She'd nod her head, this time with a smile. And I'd end with, "And I love you forever, for always, and no matter what!" With a giggle and a hug, she was off and ready for her next challenge.

Ariana is now four and a half. We've continued "come see me" time for scraped knees and bruised feelings, for "good mornings" and "good nights."

A few weeks ago, I had "one of those days." I was tired, cranky, and overextended taking care of a four-year-old, twin teenage boys, and a home business. Each phone call or knock at the door brought another full day's worth of work that needed to be done immediately! I reached my breaking point in the afternoon and went into my room for a good cry.

Ariana soon came to my side and said, "Come see me." She curled up beside me, put her sweet little hands on my damp cheeks and said,

"Are you my mommy?" Between my tears I nodded my head yes. "My sweetie, beetie mommy?" I nodded my head and smiled. "And I love you forever, for always, and no matter what!" A giggle, a big hug, and I was off and ready for my next challenge.

— Jeanette Lisefski
Chicken Soup for the Mother's Soul

*Make a memory
with your children,
spend some time to
show you care;
toys and trinkets can't
replace those precious
moments that you share.*

ELAINE HARDT

An Indescribable Gift

She slips into this world, and
into my arms, placed there by heaven.
She is straight from God. An indescribable gift. As I look upon her, peace and
purity fill the air around her. Through
joyful tears I whisper in her ear, "We are

glad you are here. We waited so long to see you." She opens her eyes, and I am transformed—a timeless moment filled with the infinity of what life is. In her eyes I see total recognition, unconditional love and complete trust. I am a mother. In that instant I feel, and in my heart I know, everything I need to know to guide her.

Lying on the bed, she sleeps between her daddy and me. We count the toes and fingers and marvel at the

perfection in such a tiny form. We look
for ways she looks like us, and ways she
is uniquely herself. We have nothing to
say, but our hearts and minds are full of
thoughts — of our hopes and dreams for
her, of who she might be, of what gifts
she brings with her and how she might
touch the world. Just looking at her and
feeling the love and sweetness she brings,
it seems the stress and weight of the
world are lifted from us, and what is
important and true in the world becomes

apparent — as being in the presence of a great, wise sage. It is hard to close our eyes to sleep.

As the days and years pass, we are awed at the transformation of who she is becoming. The first smile, the first word, the first step — all according to plan, yet in her own time and special way. She teaches us how to play again; to slow down and see the world again. To rediscover the things we used to see, and know. It is clear there is much she remembers, feels and sees that we no longer can, and maybe never could.

Time will fly; suddenly she will be grown, a young adult, ready to soar into the world and give what she came here for. Letting go will be wrenching, and yet we know that she is not ours to keep. She came to us to teach us our lessons, to give us joy, to make us whole and to connect us to God.

— *Jeanette Lisefski*
Chicken Soup for the Mother's Soul

All Those Years

My friend Debbie's two daughters were in high school when she experienced severe flu-like symtoms. Debbie visited her family doctor, who told her the flu bug had passed her by. Instead, she had been touched by the "love bug" and was now pregnant.

The birth of Tommy, a healthy, beautiful son was an event for celebration, and as time went by, it seemed as though every day brought another reason to celebrate the gift

of Tommy's life. He was sweet,
thoughtful, fun-loving and a joy
to be around.

One day when Tommy was
about five years old, he and Debbie
were driving to the neighborhood
mall. As is the way with children,
out of nowhere, Tommy asked,
"Mom how old were you when I
was born?"

"Thirty-six, Tommy. Why?"
Debbie asked, wondering what his

little mind was contemplating.

"What a shame!" Tommy responded.

"What do you mean?" Debbie inquired, more than a little puzzled. Looking at her with love-filled eyes, Tommy said, "Just think of all those years we didn't know each other."

— *ALICE COLLINS*
  Chicken Soup for the Mother's Soul

The Unlocked Door

In Glasgow, Scotland, a young lady, like a lot of teens today, got tired of home and the restraints of her parents. The daughter rejected her family's religious lifestyle and said, "I don't want your God. I give up. I'm leaving!"

She left home, deciding to become a woman of the world. Before long, however, she was dejected and unable to find a job, so she took to the streets to sell her body as a

prostitute. The years passed by,
her father died, her mother grew
older and the daughter became
more and more entrenched in her
way of life.

No contact was made between
mother and daughter during these
years. The mother, having heard of
her daughter's whereabouts, made her
way to the skid-row section of the city
in search of her daughter. She stopped
at each of the rescue missions with a

simple request. "Would you allow me to put up this picture?" It was a picture of the smiling, gray-haired mother with a handwritten message at the bottom: "I love you still... come home!"

Some more months went by, and nothing happened. Then one day the daughter wandered into the rescue mission for a needed meal. She sat absent-mindedly listening to the service, all the while letting her eyes wander over to the bulletin board. There she saw the picture and thought, *Could that be my mother?*

She couldn't wait until the service was over. She stood and went to look. It was her mother, and there were those words, "I love you still... come home!" As she stood in front of the picture, she wept. It was too good to be true.

By this time it was night, but

she was so touched by the message
that she started walking home.
When she arrived it was early in
the morning. She was afraid and
made her way timidly, not really
knowing what to do. As she knocked,
the door flew open on its own. She
thought someone must have broken
into the house. Concerned for her
mother's safety, the young woman
ran to the bedroom and found her
awake and said, "It's me! It's me!

I'm home!"

The mother couldn't believe her eyes. She wiped her tears and they fell into each other's arms. The daughter said, "I was so worried! The door was open and I thought someone had broken in!"

The mother replied gently, "No, dear. From the day you left, that door has never been locked."

— *Robert Strand*
Chicken Soup for the Mother's Soul

When you were small
And just a touch away,
I covered you with blankets
Against the cool night air.
But now that you are tall
And out of reach,
I fold my hands
And cover you with prayer.

DONA MADDUX COOPER

The Inspection

The scouts were in camp. In an inspection, the director found an umbrella neatly rolled inside the bedroll of a small scout. As an umbrella was not listed as a necessary item, the director asked the boy to explain.

"Sir," answered the young man with a weary sigh, "did you ever have a mother?"

— Author Unknown
  Submitted by Glenn Van Ekeren
  Chicken Soup for the Mother's Soul

I Don't Want a New Baby

"I don't want a new baby."

This was my oldest son Brian's response when I told him his father and I were expecting a third child. We'd survived the first round of sibling rivalry when his brother, Damian, was born. But now three-year-old Brian had made his stand about this new baby, and neither logic, reason, nor persuasion could budge him.

Puzzled, I asked him,
"Why don't you want a new baby?"
With wide and teary eyes,
he looked straight at me and said,
"Because I want to keep Damian."

— *Rosemary Laurey*
  Chicken Soup for the Mother's Soul

Every child born
into the world is a
new thought of God,
an ever-fresh and
radiant possibility.

Kate Douglas Wiggin

My Daughter,
My Teacher

Children teach us something every day. As a parent, I have learned to expect this. Yet sometimes the extent of what my daughter teaches surprises me.

When Marissa was six months old, it seemed she was always looking up. As I gazed upward with her, I learned the magic of leaves dancing on trees and the awesome size of the tail of a jet. At eight months she was

forever looking down. I learned that
each stone is different, sidewalk cracks
make intricate designs and blades
of grass come in a variety of greens.

   Then she turned 11 months
and began saying "Wow!" She spoke
this marvelous word for anything
new and wonderful to her, such as
the assortment of toys she spotted
in the pediatrician's office or the
gathering of clouds before a storm.

She whispered, "Oh, wow!" for things that really impressed her, like a brisk breeze on her face or a flock of geese honking overhead. Then there was the ultimate in "Wow," a mouthing of the word with no sound, reserved for truly awesome events. These included the sunset on a lake after a magnificent day in Minnesota and fireworks in the summer sky.

She has taught me many

ways to say "I love you." She said
it well one morning when she was
14 months old. We were cuddling.
She buried her head in my shoulder
and with a sigh of contentment said
"Happy." Another day (during her
terrific twos) she pointed to a beautiful
model on the cover of a magazine
and said, "Is that you, Mom?" Most
recently my now three-year-old walked
into the kitchen while I was cleaning

up after supper and said, "Can I help?" Shortly after this she put her hand on my arm and said, "Mom, if you were a kid, we'd be friends."

At moments like this, all I can say is, "Oh, wow!"

— *Janet S. Meyer*
  Chicken Soup for the Mother's Soul

A Child's Vision

My child took a crayon
In her little hand
And started to draw
As if by command.

I looked on with pleasure
But couldn't foresee
What the few simple lines
Were going to be.

What are you drawing?
I asked, by and by.
I'm making a picture
Of God in the sky.

But nobody knows
What God looks like, I sighed.
They will when I'm finished
She calmly replied.

— *Sherwin Kaufman*
  Chicken Soup for the Mother's Soul

Mother love is the fuel that enables a normal human being to do the impossible.

MARION C. GARRETTY

Angel in Uniform

Where there is great love there are always miracles.

Willa Cather

This is a family story my father told me about his mother, my grandmother.

In 1949, my father had just returned home from the war. On every American highway you could see soldiers in uniform hitchhiking home to their families, as was the custom at that time in America.

Sadly, the thrill of his reunion with his family was soon overshadowed. My grandmother became very ill and had to be hospitalized. It was her kidneys, and the doctors told my father that she needed a blood transfusion immediately or she would not live through the night. The problem was that Grandmother's blood type was AB-, a very rare type even today, but even harder to get then because there were no blood banks or air flights to ship blood. All the family members were typed, but not one member was a match. So the doctors gave the family no hope; my grandmother was dying.

My father left the hospital in tears to gather up all the family members, so that everyone would get a chance to tell Grandmother good-bye. As my father was driving down the highway, he passed a soldier in uniform hitchhiking home to his family. Deep in grief, my father had no inclination at

that moment to do a good deed. Yet
it was almost as if something outside
himself pulled him to a stop, and he
waited as the stranger climbed into the car.

My father was too upset to even
ask the soldier his name, but the soldier
noticed my father's tears right away and
inquired about them. Through his tears,
my father told this total stranger that his
mother was lying in a hospital dying
because the doctors had been unable to
locate her blood type, AB-, and if they

did not locate her blood type before nightfall, she would surely die.

It got very quiet in the car. Then this unidentified soldier extended his hand out to my father, palm up. Resting in the palm of his hand were the dog tags from around his neck. The blood type on the tags was AB-. The soldier told my father to turn the car around and get him to the hospital.

My grandmother lived until 1996, 47 years later, and to this day no one in our family knows the soldier's name. But my father has often wondered, was he a soldier or an angel in uniform?

— *Jeannie Ecke Sowell*
  Chicken Soup for the Mother's Soul

There are only two lasting
bequests we can hope to give our
children. One of these is roots;
the other is wings.

HODDING CARTER

The Broken Doll

Here's a story a friend of mine once told me, in her own words:

One day my young daughter was late coming home from school. I was both annoyed and worried. When she came through the door, I demanded in my upset tone that she explain why she was late.

She said, "Mommy, I was walking home with Julie and halfway home Julie dropped her doll and it broke into lots of little pieces."

"Oh, honey," I replied, "you were late because you helped Julie pick up the pieces of her doll to put them back together."

In her young and innocent voice, my daughter said, "No, Mommy. I didn't know how to fix the doll. I just stayed to help Julie cry."

— *Dan Clark*
Chicken Soup for the Mother's Soul

$\mathcal{A}$ mother's love is
like a circle, it has no beginning
and no ending. It keeps going around
and around ever expanding, touching
everyone who comes in contact with it.
Engulfing them like the morning's mist,
warming them like the noontime sun,
and covering them like a blanket
of evening stars.

ART URBAN

The Signs of
Advanced Momhood

Maybe it starts when you realize rock concerts give you a headache. Or that you're offering to cut up other people's food. Or you catch yourself ending a discussion with, "Because I'm the mother, that's why."

You've reached a new level of motherhood. All the warning signs are there. You know you've crossed the threshold into advanced mommydom when:

* You count the sprinkles on each kid's cupcake to make sure they're equal.

* You have time to shave only one leg.

* You hide in the bathroom to be alone.

* Your child throws up and you catch it.

* Someone else's kid throws up at a party and you keep eating.

* Your child insists that you read *Once Upon a Potty* out loud in the lobby of Grand Central Terminal, and you do it.

— *Liane Kupferberg Carter*
  Chicken Soup for the Mother's Soul